I'M SO HUNGRY

AND OTHER PLAYS

**LEARNING
MEDIA®**

Distributed in the United States of America by Celebration Press,
10 Bank Street, White Plains, NY 10606-5026

Published 1999 by Learning Media Limited,
Box 3293, Wellington 6001, New Zealand

10 9 8 7 6 5 4 3 2 1

Printed in Hong Kong

ISBN 0 478 22906 2

Contents

The BUS Kids

by Jan Trafford
illustrated by Geoffrey Notman

Characters

PRINCIPAL (MISS PRINGLE)   AMY
OTHER CHILDREN   BRENT
BUS MONITOR   TWINS
EDDIE

PRINCIPAL. I'd like all the bus pupils to stay behind after assembly, please. The rest of you may go quietly back to your classes.

    OTHER CHILDREN *go out.*

BUS MONITOR. Uh-oh, someone's squealed on us. There goes my bus monitor's badge!

PRINCIPAL. Now, is everyone here?

EDDIE. It wasn't me, Miss Pringle. Honest!

AMY. I was sitting at the front. So it can't have been me!

BRENT. I ate all my lunch before the bus came. There wasn't any food in my lunchbox. So it can't have been me!

TWINS. We went to sleep on the bus yesterday. And the day before. So it wasn't us!

PRINCIPAL. OK! OK! Settle down, please. I need to talk to all of you about …

EDDIE. I didn't even have gum on the bus this week.

AMY. Nor did I … or candy ….

BRENT. The window where I was sitting was jammed. So I couldn't have thrown anything out anyway!

BUS MONITOR. I know – it's the mice, isn't it?

TWINS. But we didn't let them out in the bus this week. We kept them in our lunchboxes.

PRINCIPAL. I've asked you to stay behind because …

EDDIE. I didn't cut the back of the seat – it's always been like that.

TWINS, BRENT, AMY, *and* **EDDIE** (*all together*). We're in trouble, aren't we?

BUS MONITOR. Just be quiet, all of you!
Listen to Miss Pringle. Let's hear what she
has to say!

All of the bus pupils are quiet.

PRINCIPAL. Ah, that's better. I had no idea so
many interesting things happened on the
school bus!

BUS MONITOR. So we aren't in trouble?

PRINCIPAL. Well, the bus driver called me
this morning …

BUS MONITOR. Uh-oh, here we go …!

PRINCIPAL. … and she says that from next Monday, you'll all be traveling on a brand new bus! With heaters that work!

TWINS. You mean no more breakdowns?

PRINCIPAL. No more breakdowns!

BRENT. Windows that open?

PRINCIPAL. Of course.

EDDIE. Seats without holes in them?

PRINCIPAL. That's right.

ALL. Yahoo! At last! A new bus!

PRINCIPAL. Yes! Great news, isn't it? Now, maybe you could think up some rules about how to look after your lovely new bus. What do you think?

TWINS. No pet mice!

BRENT. No throwing things out the window!

EDDIE. No chewing gum under the seats!

AMY. No candy papers!

BUS MONITOR. And always be nice to the bus monitor!

Everyone groans.

9

Fishy

by Bill Nagelkerke
illustrated by Philip Webb

CHARACTERS

MARK	DOG
ANNA	DAD
POLLY	MOM

SCENE: **MARK**, **ANNA**, and **POLLY** *are standing in the kitchen. They have their backs to the fridge. The fridge door is open, and inside is a string of "sausages" on a plate.*

MARK. Someone's stolen my chocolate marshmallow fish. It was in the fridge this morning beside the sausages. I saved it to have after school.

ANNA. Yuck! Who'd want a chocolate marshmallow fish smelling of sausages?

MARK. Someone did.

ANNA. Maybe you ate it yourself.

MARK. I didn't!

POLLY. Don't cry. I'll find out who it was. (*She picks up a pen and writing pad.*) If Mark didn't eat the chocolate fish himself, that leaves Mom, Dad, or you, Anna.

She writes down the names.

ANNA. What if it was a burglar?

POLLY. A burglar would have taken the video player as well.

ANNA. Well, it wasn't me!

POLLY. Prove it!

ANNA. Mark and I watched TV together before we went to bed. He knows I didn't go near the fridge. So there!

POLLY (*to* **MARK**). Is that right?

> **MARK** *nods.* **POLLY** *crosses* **ANNA'S**
> *name off the list.*

POLLY. It can't have been Dad.

MARK. Why not?

POLLY. Because Dad can't eat chocolate. He gets zits.

> **POLLY** *crosses* **DAD'S** *name off the list.*

MARK. You're a good detective. Dad hasn't got zits, so it can't have been him.

ANNA. Anyone could have worked that out.

> **DAD** *comes into the kitchen.*

DAD. What's going on?

ANNA. Someone's stolen Mark's chocolate fish.

POLLY. I'm finding out who did it. It wasn't you, Dad.

DAD. I know it wasn't. Now clear the way, you guys. I've got to get a meal ready before Mom comes home.

> **POLLY** and **ANNA** *nod.* **MARK** *moves to one side. The fridge door stays open.*
>
> **DAD** *bustles about preparing tea.*

POLLY. It wasn't Dad, and it wasn't Mom either.

ANNA. Why not?

POLLY. Because it was Mom who gave us the fish in the first place.

She crosses **MOM'S** *name off the list.*

ANNA. I know who took Mark's fish. (*She points at* **POLLY**.) It was you!

POLLY. Prove it!

ANNA. Yours is the only name that's not crossed off.

POLLY (*crossing off her name*). Now it is.

ANNA. Well, prove that it wasn't you!

POLLY. Easy peasy! I was at ballet class last night, and Mom made me go to bed as soon as we got home.

> **MOM** *arrives home from work. Without anyone on stage noticing, the dog sneaks into the kitchen and runs off with the sausages from the fridge.*

MARK (*to* **MOM**). I want my chocolate fish! Someone's stolen it!

MOM. Oh dear! I hoped you wouldn't see that it was gone.

ANNA. Mom did take it!

MOM. I didn't have time for breakfast this morning, so I munched Mark's fish on my way to work. I've bought you another one.

She hands **MARK** *a chocolate marshmallow fish.* **MARK** *eats it.*

POLLY. I knew it was one of us!

MARK. I'm still hungry.

POLLY. So am I. It's hard work being a detective.

ANNA. When's supper ready?

DAD (*looking in the fridge*). Who's stolen the sausages?

The dog runs back across the kitchen, trailing the sausages behind him.

The Magic Wand

by Philippa Werry

illustrations by
Jenny Cooper

Characters

MISS PERFECT
KATIE
JOE
1ST CHILD
2ND CHILD
DIFFERENT BOY
CHILDREN
3RD CHILD
PRINCIPAL

SCENE: *A classroom. All the children are making lots of noise and throwing paper darts.*

MISS PERFECT. Quiet, everyone! (*The class quietens down.*) I've never known such a noisy class! The principal is coming to visit us today, so you'll have to behave. Katie, stop waving that stick around.

KATIE. It's not a stick, Miss Perfect, it's a magic wand.

MISS PERFECT. A magic wand? I'm afraid magic wands don't really exist, Katie.

KATIE. This *is* a magic wand. My dad made it for me.

MISS PERFECT. Now then, that's enough. I'll look after this stick until the end of school. Quiet, everyone! I want you all reading nicely when the principal comes.

KATIE. Please may I have my magic wand back?

MISS PERFECT (*waving the wand around*). No, Katie, I'm going to look after it for you.

KATIE. Well, just be careful then.

MISS PERFECT. Be careful? Why? Quiet, everyone! Joe, if you really want to jump around like a kangaroo, I just wish ...

KATIE. Don't say I didn't warn you!

MISS PERFECT. I just wish you'd go and be a kangaroo outside.

   JOE, *looking very surprised, turns into a kangaroo and goes hopping outside.*

MISS PERFECT. What on earth ...?

KATIE. See, I told you.

MISS PERFECT. You mean it really is a ...? No, it can't be. Joe's just pretending to be a kangaroo.

1ST CHILD. No, Miss Perfect, he really has turned into a kangaroo. You should see the huge jumps he's doing around the playground.

2ND CHILD. Please turn him back, Miss Perfect. He doesn't look very happy.

MISS PERFECT. All right, then, but how do I do it?

KATIE. Just wish, that's all.

MISS PERFECT. Ah ... I wish ... I wish ... I wish Joe would turn into a boy again.

A **DIFFERENT BOY** *comes into the classroom and goes to sit down at* **JOE'S** *desk.*

CHILDREN. That's not Joe!

KATIE. No, Miss Perfect, you didn't do it right. You've turned him back into a different boy.

MISS PERFECT (*flustered*). Oh dear, oh dear. I wish ... I wish ...

KATIE (*taking wand*). Let me do it. I wish that this boy would go outside and turn back into Joe again.

> **DIFFERENT BOY** *goes outside, and* **JOE** *comes back in.*

CHILDREN. Hooray!

MISS PERFECT. Well, I never! Goodness me! All right, class, quiet, please! Hmmm. I've got an idea. (*She takes the wand back again.*) I wish you would all sit and be as quiet as mice!

> *All the children sit down in silence until ...*

CHILDREN. Squeak! Squeak! Squeak!

MISS PERFECT. No, no, that's not what I meant at all. When the principal comes in, I wish you would all be as quiet as **QUIET**!

*The **CHILDREN** are sitting absolutely silent when the principal comes in.*

PRINCIPAL. Hello, Miss Perfect. Hello, class.

There is no reply.

PRINCIPAL. What very quiet children! Are they real?

MISS PERFECT. Ha, ha. Yes, they're certainly real.

*The **PRINCIPAL** walks around the classroom, peering over the children's heads at the books they are reading.*

PRINCIPAL. Very interesting. Quite astonishing. You certainly seem to have worked magic with these children, Miss Perfect.

MISS PERFECT. Thank you, Principal.

PRINCIPAL (*going out shaking her head*). Thank you, Miss Perfect. Goodbye. Goodbye, class.

3RD CHILD. Please, Miss Perfect, would you unwish us? It's terribly hard work being so quiet.

MISS PERFECT. Well, I suppose so, but it's very nice and peaceful like this.

3RD CHILD. Please, Miss Perfect.

KATIE. Just make sure you do it right, that's all.

MISS PERFECT. All right. Now then, I wish this class was all back to normal.

> *The* **CHILDREN** *cheer, and everyone except* **KATIE** *runs outside.*

KATIE. Now can I have my magic wand back?

MISS PERFECT. Well, actually, Katie, I think I'm going to hold onto this stick of yours a little while longer – just to be on the safe side!

SCENE: **DAD**, **TESSA**, *and* **JOSH** *come into the fast-food restaurant. Some* **OTHER PEOPLE** *are already sitting eating at the tables.*

TESSA. Hurry up, Dad. I'm starving.

JOSH. I'm so hungry, I could eat a horse.

DAD. Let's hope you won't have to do that.

TESSA. Come on – what are we going to have?

DAD. Let's see what they've got.

They go over to the counter.

COOK. Hello, there.

DAD. Hello. Let's see – we'd like three pies.

COOK. Certainly. We've got snail pies or worm pies.

DAD. Wha-at?

TESSA. Snail pies, yuk!

JOSH. Worm pies, gross!

COOK. What's wrong with a nice juicy worm pie?

27

DAD. Don't you have any ordinary sort of pies?

COOK. What do you mean, ordinary?

DAD. Well, like apple or blueberry?

COOK. Apple! Blueberry! Ugh!

DAD. All right, let's forget about the pies. Have you got any fried chicken?

COOK. Fried chicken? Certainly not! Where do you people come from!

DAD. Down south. We're just passing through on vacation.

COOK. Well, remind me never to go down south when I go on vacation. We've got fried toads' legs or fried lizards' tails.

TESSA. Fried toads' legs!

JOSH. Fried lizards' tails!

COOK. Yes, they're delicious. That's what the people over there are having.

DAD. Perhaps we could just have dessert.

COOK. Certainly.

DAD. You *must* have ice cream.

COOK. Of course we've got ice cream. You can have Double …

TESSA. Double Chocolate?

COOK. Double Mud or Super Special …

JOSH. Super Special Strawberry?

COOK. Super Special Slime.

DAD. I don't believe this. I think I'll just have a drink. Coffee for me, please.

COOK. We don't have coffee.

DAD (*shouting*). Well, what *do* you have?

COOK. Hot sloppy slush or cold ice sludge. And freshly squeezed onion juice for the kids.

DAD. Somehow, I don't feel hungry any more.

JOSH. Well, I do.

TESSA. Me too.

JOSH. I'm going to try a snail pie. Those people over there are eating them.

TESSA. I'll have a worm one.

JOSH. Can I try some of yours?

DAD. I feel a bit sick. I think I'll just go outside for a minute and get some fresh air.

TESSA. Poor Dad. Come and have something to eat when you feel a bit better.

JOSH. These pies look great.

TESSA. Where shall we sit?

JOSH. There's a table over there.

TESSA. Let's eat, then. I'm so hungry, I could …

JOSH and **TESSA** (*together*). …

EAT A HORSE!

illustrated by Lorenzo Van Der Lingen